TALENT NIGHT

by Linda B. Ross
illustrated by Jackie Snider

Harcourt

Orlando   Boston   Dallas   Chicago   San Diego

Visit *The Learning Site!*

www.harcourtschool.com

Ben Bird and Fern Fox had a plan. They were going to plan a talent night!

"We'll all perform!" said Ben
Bird. "It will be terrific!"

The animals planned their acts. Ben Bird wanted to sing. Fern Fox wanted to twirl.

Sal felt hurt. "I don't sing or twirl," she said. "I can't do these things!"

"Oh, well! I'll gather some nuts," she said. So Sal went on her way to find nuts for dinner.

Sal found four nuts under a plant. She hummed as she picked them up.

Soon her basket was full. "I'll follow the path to my house," said Sal.

Sal hummed on her way
home. Ben Bird was
perched on a branch.

"You are terrific, Sal!"
called Ben and Fern. "Will
you perform with us?"

"Oh, yes, Ben and Fern!
I will perform with you."

So Ben Bird sang. Fern Fox twirled. Sal Squirrel hummed. They were perfect!